Mona Minim
and the Smell of the Sun

JANET FRAME

Mona Minim

and the Smell of the Sun

Illustrated by ROBIN JACQUES

GEORGE BRAZILLER   New York

Acknowledgments

As this small book was written in the United States I'd like to acknowledge the hospitality I received there. Grateful thanks to George and Marsha Braziller, Edwin Seaver, Bertie Hoover, Helen Dressner, Sue and John Marquand in New York and John Money in Baltimore; the Yaddo Foundation; the Henry Foundation; and Carl Brandt for his interest.

A story for Pamela in Auckland
and James in New York

Contents

Mona Minim
and the Smell of the Sun

1. The First Journey

*O*nce upon a time, not long ago, almost now, there was a young House Ant called Mona Minim who was preparing to make her first journey out of the nest.

"Mona Minim!"

Aunt Theodora, the old blind nurse-ant, was waiting. The eggs were chosen, and each ant knew which egg it would care for and turn in the sun, and when was play-time and when was rest-time. The small group of youngest ants was gathered excitedly in the trail that led from the nest in the garage roof, up through the kitchen floor, inside the kitchen cupboard, under the kitchen door to the stairs.

"Mona Minim!" Aunt Theodora called impatiently.

Mona was still in her bedroom combing her long black plaits, making herself pretty for her first journey into the sunlight. She looked at her reflection in the shining beetle-back mirror that hung on the wall. Then she put on her yellow sunbonnet, smoothed her best floral apron where it was creased, rubbed a little more polish into her six black-buttoned shoes, and hurried from the bedroom.

"Coming, Aunt Theodora!"

It was no use hoping that Aunt Theodora wouldn't notice you were missing. It was no use thinking that because she was blind you could creep up afterward when you had finished your toilet. Sometimes it seemed that Aunt Theodora knew everything about everything and everybody. If you went into her tiny room at the top of the trail leading down to the Underground Garden you could see pinned on the walls every ribbon and medal she had ever won for Sense, Recognition, Communication. And she had won many. But if you looked closely you could see that most of the medals and ribbons were from the days when she was young, and she was old now, so old that no one in the colony remembered her arrival, if she had been born there or had come from Outside or how she had come to be there at all. She was just Aunt Theodora the nursemaid, as much a part of the life of the House Ants as their nest in the garage roof beneath the kitchen of the House.

Mona Minim believed that Aunt Theodora had always been old. She just used to sit there looking after the eggs and the youngest ants while she knitted in fancy patterns, woolen wing-covers for the Princess, and once when Mona Minim said, "Aunt Theodora have you ever had wings and been flying?" Aunt Theodora looked sad at first and then she laughed a loud laugh, "What would I want with wings? Who would ever want to fly?"

Then Mona Minim thought but did not like to ask her, What is the smell of the sky when you are flying, and the smell of the wind that never comes close to the earth, and of the clouds? What is the smell of the sun?

"Mona Minim! At last!"

As she ran by the bakehouse Mona sneaked in, grabbed a slice of bread, wrapped it in her lawn handkerchief, tucked her handkerchief in her pocket, and making sure that no one had observed her she hurried toward the cluster of waiting ants. Eagerly she touched *ant*ennae with her closest friend, Pamela, who had been three times outside the nest. And then she told Aunt Theodora she was sorry for being late but as this was her first journey into the sunlight she had wanted to dress in her best clothes. How hurt she felt when Aunt Theodora seemed angry!

"It's wiser for you to dress like the others on your first day, Mona. The smell of your floral apron and your yellow sunbonnet and your six black-buttoned shoes (how did Aunt Theodora *know* when she was blind?) is not your usual smell. Remember what happened to Cousin Bruno."

Oh, Mona thought wearily. Could anyone ever forget what had happened to Cousin Bruno? The older ants were always frightening the young ants with the story of Cousin Bruno who had been caught and killed by his own family simply because he was wearing a different smell in his clothing.

Suddenly Mona felt scared and strange dressed in her floral apron and yellow sunbonnet and black-buttoned shoes. She knew that ants detecting an unfamiliar smell become fierce and hostile. She had known the feeling herself when strange scent-waves trembled across her *ant*ennae.

Aunt Theodora, watching her, sensing her fears, said more kindly, "Because it's your first day out, Mona, you can wear your best clothes, but remember it's not wise. And I'll let you carry one egg and when we're out on the trail and have found a place in the sun you can turn and sun the egg all by yourself."

How proud Mona felt! "Can Pamela come with me, and we'll play our special Stair Game?"

"Of course," Aunt Theodora said, happy now that the journey had begun and every ant was moving forward.

"We're coming home for tea," she reminded them. "We haven't taken a picnic basket."

Mona smiled to herself, thinking of the slice of bread wrapped in her lawn handkerchief. She and Pamela would share it after they had sunbathed the eggs and played the Stair Game which Mona had heard so much about and had never played, and were resting wherever it was that ants rested when they were away from home.

At the thought of being away from home Mona shivered. She'd heard others talk of going outside the nest for the first time, and she'd talked of it too, and dreamed of it, and longed for the day to come. And now it was here.

Overwhelmed by the prospect of Outside, Mona stopped in her trail. Pamela, next in line, touched her *ant*ennae.

"You're shivering," she whispered.

Mona was glad she didn't say aloud, Mona Minim, you're scared.

"I shivered like that too, on my first journey," Pamela said with just enough superiority to let it be known that she had been three times out of the nest.

Mona said nothing to that. The egg was beginning to feel heavy but she would never have dared to admit it. How she longed to stop for a rest, just once!

And then they saw it. Mona saw it and everyone saw it. It was the entrance to the nest with two big-headed soldier ants guarding it. Mona had never been as far as this in her life, in her whole life.

Closing her eyes she said to herself, in three breaths, or four breaths or five, I shall be outside in the sun. When I open my eyes I shall be there.

Six breaths later she opened her eyes.

2. "Is This the Sunlight?"

*F*or a moment she felt dizzy, as if she were going to fall. There was so much light everywhere and so many new smells that she didn't know which way to turn. Pamela came up to her.

"I felt like that too," she said, again with just enough superiority to let it be known that she was used to Outside and Sunlight.

Mona had to confess to herself that she was glad when Pamela said thoughtfully, "I'll go ahead of you now and you follow. It's not far to the Stairs."

The Stairs and the Stair Game!

It seemed to Mona that all her life she had longed to play the famous Stair Game, and now she was out, Outside, ready to play it for the first time.

Struck by a sudden dizzying rush of light she staggered and fell on the trail. Pamela stopped to help her.

"Is this the sun striking me?" Mona asked. "Is this the sunlight trying to topple me over every few steps I take and sucking my eyes into the big fire, to blind them? Is this the sunlight yellow like my sunbonnet?"

"Something like," Pamela said, trying to sound wise, for she was not very much older than Mona and she did not really know how to explain the sunlight.

"What's Aunt Theodora stopping for? What's she saying to the scouts? How far is it to the Stairs?"

The news spread quickly. The scouts were worried about the strange smell —Mona's smell in her floral apron and yellow sunbonnet and her black-buttoned shoes; and perhaps the slice of bread wrapped in her lawn handkerchief.

Mona felt that almost every ant had turned to stare at her. She could not help feeling proud. It was her first journey Outside and her smell was different and who cared what had happened to Cousin Bruno? How reckless and dizzy and adventurous Mona felt. Oh Oh to reach the stairs! Oh Oh to play the Stair Game! She was so excited she was not sure she would remember how to play the Stair Game. She was so excited that she did not even stop, as Pamela did, to have a drink of honey from the public stomach of one of the workers who was hurrying home to the nest.

"There's nothing I like better than fresh honey," Pamela said, trying to sound grownup.

"There's nothing I like better than playing the Stair Game in the sunlight," Mona answered, feeling a bit tipsy.

She knew it was the most wonderful game in the world, as all games are that are dreamed of and dreamed of and practiced in imagination long before they are played. Oh it was only a simple tiggy and touch and hide and seek and swing but it was also Daylight and Sunlight and being grownup enough to venture beyond the nest, and planning how to spend your life and wondering what it was like to be a Princess and fly close to the smell of the sun. It was not being afraid of the bullying scouts or of what had happened to Cousin Bruno, or of seeing the Queen or of dropping the eggs or of being alone in the egg chamber when the glowworm light went out. Oh Oh the Stair Game! Oh Oh the sunlight!

Suddenly Mona noticed that the ants seemed to be resting. Pamela was sitting there lounging as if she were the Queen herself with the egg beside her and the sun hitting her over the head with its strong yellow smell that had white streaks like snow and a wet touch on one side and a burning touch on the other with the smell of danger blowing in a vapor between.

"Why have we stopped?" Mona asked, secretly thankful they had decided to rest. "How far is it to the Stairs?"

This time Pamela really spoke in a superior way. "This is it, silly. We're here. We're Outside on the Stairs."

What happened next was always confusing in Mona's memory. Whether it was her disappointment or her disbelief or her impatience with Pamela she did not know but reaching impulsively forward to pull at Pamela's plaits that were long and black like her own she found herself in a nothingness, like falling, and the last she heard was Pamela's tiny frightened voice:

"Aunt Theodora. Aunt Theodora. Mona Minim has fallen down a crack in the stairs."

3. *Through the*

Sunflower Forest

*W*hen Mona woke up it was dark and she felt stiff and sick and cold and very frightened. She was afraid to move in case the darkness heard her and touched her, crushing her, or seized her between its jaws. She discovered she had fallen in a soft place as soft as the woolen wing-covers that Aunt Theodora knitted for the Princess, or the blankets she stitched for the larvae.

Aunt Theodora!

Mona remembered. She was Outside. She had fallen through a crack in the Stairs. The nest was far away, the nest and Aunt Theodora and Pamela and the tunnels and the egg-chamber where she went after infant school to help with the eggs and the new babies; all were so far away. She longed for her little bed with the aphis-green coverlet and the thistledown pillow and the beetle-back mirror hanging on the wall; and the honey and bread and crackle-and-damp-whisper smell of home. Once or twice she thought of Cousin Bruno but she tried not to, oh she tried not to. And then because she was only a little ant and this was her first journey outside the nest and she'd wanted so much to play the Stair Game and she was lonely with

the sun gone away and everything dark, she began to cry, waving her *ant*ennae in confusion as she tried to cope with all the new fearful smells that said Danger.

But her *ant*ennae were tired and she herself was tired because she was only a little ant on her first journey outside the nest.

She cried herself to sleep.

When she woke she was still safe and for a moment she wondered where she was lying. She was bathed warm in a morning sun and she was hungry. There was no sign of any other members of the colony. Would they not have sent scouts to search for her? Surely she was not so very far from the nest? Oh what a tale she would tell when at last she was safely home!

Confidently now, just waiting to be rescued, and feeling so warm and cosy in the sun, she sat eating a delicious breakfast—the slice of bread that she'd wrapped in her lawn handkerchief and put in the pocket of her floral apron.

And when she'd finished that she drank two sweet dewdrops that were caught in the folds of her yellow sunbonnet. Then she cleaned herself well, making sure the scent-cones of her *ant*ennae were free for perfect reception, though one had been hurt in her fall and was swollen and if she'd been at home Aunt Theodora or one of the nurse-ants would have exclaimed, "Dear me, Mona Minim, a swollen scent-cone. Off to bed with you."

And they would have put her to bed and drawn up the aphis-green coverlet to keep her warm, and brought her honey to sip, and old Aunty Reepy who was always full of honey would have come whenever Mona called, to feed her and nurse her until her scent-cone had healed.

Mona was beginning to feel unhappy again, thinking of home, when she smelt something moving nearby and before she had time to decide what to do a small black ant appeared. Sensing her it sprang back and waved its *ant*ennae and arched its abdomen in the defense-attack position, and Mona could see that its jaws were opening to grab her. All she could do was plead in her small-ant voice,

"Don't eat me. I'm Mona Minim on my first journey out of the nest. Please don't eat me."

The stranger assumed a more friendly posture.

"I'm Barbara. This is my second day out of the nest. My cousin Nigel is going to marry the Princess one day. What are you doing on my trail?"

Mona was envious.

"Did you make this trail all by yourself on your first day?"

"Of course. We garden ants are educated. And you've been sleeping in my rest-bed. I made that myself too."

Then Barbara came and sat on the bed beside Mona and they found they were almost the same age and Mona told Barbara about Aunt Theodora and Pamela and the Stair Game and what had happened to Cousin Bruno, and Barbara told Mona about her Aunt Phyllis and her Uncle Pogo and her cousin Nigel who was going to marry a Princess; and the Garden Ant nest; and the Sunflower Forest—oh there were so many things to talk about!

"Just fancy, we're almost the same age," Mona said.

"But I'm a Garden Ant," Barbara said proudly. "And I'm found. And you're only a House Ant and you're lost."

Then Barbara became so bossy that Mona almost didn't like her.

"You know what will happen if they find you on our trail," Barbara warned. "They'll kill you."

Mona almost burst into tears. "But this is only my first day out of the nest. I'm Mona Minim the youngest ant. Where will I go? I'm lost and no one has found me."

"*I'm found*," Barbara said placidly. "Therefore I can find you. If I were lost I wouldn't be able to find you because I would have to find myself first. What a pity you're a House Ant, otherwise I could find you and take you home."

"I'm glad I'm a House Ant," Mona said, angrily waving her *ant*ennae. Also, Barbara's conversation confused her. "I'm glad I'm a House Ant. Look at my pretty floral apron and my black-buttoned shoes and my yellow sunbonnet, all made from remnants from the house of the people. And when you are a House Ant you can play the Stair Game."

She could see that Barbara was interested in the Stair Game. Mona, of course, did not confess that she had never played it. As she described it to Barbara, inventing and elaborating as she described, she sensed that Barbara was beginning to find it sounded just as exciting as the Garden Ant pastime of Hide and Seek in the Sunflower Forest.

"Come home with me," Barbara said suddenly. "I get so tired of Nigel and all his talk of marrying the Princess. You'll like Uncle Pogo, and Aunt Phyllis too, when you get used to her. You'll be my adopted sister. Except..."

"Except what?"

Each knew what the other was thinking. What was the use of being friends, how could you be friends if your smells were hostile?

"You know they'd kill you," Barbara said.

Mona knew that Barbara was not merely trying to frighten her. She remembered Cousin Bruno and the Sense-Recognition-Communication Studies. Even the youngest ants had to learn their S.R.C.

Mona and Barbara sat thinking hard to find a solution. If Mona stayed where she was she would almost certainly be killed. If she tried to find her way back to the House Ants she ran the same risk, through lack of experience in making trails. The only solution seemed equally perilous—to go home with Barbara, to live, a House Ant among the Garden Ants, with Aunt Phyllis and Uncle Pogo and Nigel.

And to play in the Sunflower Forest!

"If you come home with me," Barbara said, "it means that I have found you and if I ever get lost you must find me. Promise?"

Mona promised.

"I will cover you with my smell and the colony will accept you. We have lots of strange insects living peaceably with us. Oh,"—she said hastily —"not that you're *strange*. But we do have foreign species everywhere. Now you must take off your House-Ant clothes.

Sadly Mona took off her floral apron, her black-buttoned shoes, her yellow sunbonnet with the two pleats that had caught the thirst-quenching drops of honey-dew. Folding them neatly one upon the other she placed them, with the lawn handkerchief, beneath two fallen grass-blades under Barbara's rest-bed. Then she wrapped herself in a brown leaf-blanket from Mona's rest-bed while Barbara sprayed Garden Ant scent on Mona and her clothes. Instructing her to follow and not to speak if another ant spoke to her she led her along the trail through the Sunflower Forest (I did not know the sun grew on stalks, Mona could not help whispering) to the nest of the Garden Ants.

4. *Aunt Phyllis*

*C*hallenged at the entrance to the nest by two fierce-looking soldier ants, Mona stayed silent while Barbara gave her prepared reply.

"Barbara and Mona, second-day trail-makers."

The soldiers looked kindly at them. "Make sure," one of them warned, "that when you come home you clean yourself thoroughly of all the strange smells you've picked up. You'll both learn in time not to cover yourself with every smell you meet. Make sure you clean yourselves."

"I almost drew my sword, you know," the other soldier said, "when I smelt you coming along the trail. Goodness knows where you've been. But for second-day trail-makers you've done very well indeed."

Mona felt very timid as Barbara led her along tunnels and corridors past store rooms, past feeding posts where fat lantern-like ants stood motionless waiting to feed the hungry members of the colony, past a chewing society that was busily shredding a huge green leaf, to the family home where Barbara lived with Aunt Phyllis and Uncle Pogo and Nigel.

Barbara seemed very grownup, Mona thought, the way she hurried about preparing a bedroom for her newly adopted sister.

"Where's Aunt Phyllis?" Mona asked, thinking with longing of Aunt Theodora and Pamela and the Stair Game that she would never play and her own rest-bed with the thistledown pillow and the aphis-green coverlet that she would never sleep in again.

"Aunt Phyllis? Oh, she challenged us at the gate. She's a soldier."

"But she didn't seem to know you. And she didn't say Hello and tell you what was for lunch, and that...and that..." Mona said feeling very infantile.

"Oh she knew me, but her work as a soldier comes first."

"But she knows you haven't a sister? What will she say when she sees me here?"

"Don't worry. You've got my smell. Smell's all that matters. And Aunt Phyllis is always wanting me to bring someone to live here to keep me company when she's away on field operations or sentry duty. So I've brought you. Don't cry, Mona Minim. Don't be homesick. Let's have a feed of honey. And then I have to go to the nursery chamber and then I have to do one page of S.R.C. and one page of my *Ant*hology."

Mona looked admiring. "You're busier than I," she said. "But then you've been two days out of the nest. That counts, I suppose."

So they sat in the warm sitting room, sipping honey and combing their plaits and talking about what it would be like to have wings and fly, and the three things they wished for most in all the ant world, and before Mona knew it she felt drowsy and Barbara took her to her new bedroom and Mona was asleep in almost no time and only once did she wake, to see her new Aunt Phyllis bending over her, and she didn't seem a fierce soldier any more, she was kind and gentle, pulling the pretty sunflower-petal coverlet over her where she lay in bed, to keep her warm all night.

5. Spider Sandwiches

with the Crusts Cut Off

*T*he next morning Mona felt as any ant might feel in a strange place: first, she was afraid, then she thought she must be dreaming and was still inside the dream, and then she remembered what had happened. Mona might have begun to feel very homesick had not Aunt Phyllis, at that very moment, come into her bedroom with a tray on which stood a jug of nectar with its own cover of white spider-gauze anchored at each of five points around the rim by a minute fragment of preserved snowdrop; a plain whitebud cup and a plain white plate holding two spider sandwiches with the crusts cut off.

"I have to go on sentry duty," Aunt Phyllis explained. "But first I'll rub some ointment on that scent-cone of yours. We don't want you in bed sick do we?"

Putting aside the tray on the table and covering it with yet another spider-gauze cloth she proceeded to rub ointment on Mona's swollen scent-cone.

"You had better stay in bed today," she said, when she had bandaged the *ant*enna in a soft white cotton banadge. "Uncle Pogo will come to talk

to you. And Aunty Reepy will bring you a plate of fond*ant*—that's special, given only when you're sick. And we'll see how you are tomorrow."

When Aunt Phyllis had gone on sentry duty, Mona sat up in bed feeling very privileged, nibbling her spider sandwiches with the crusts cut off and drinking her warm nectar. She could hear ants bustling in the corridor out-side on their way to work or to feed or down to the nursery to look after the young ants or to the egg chamber to care for the newly born; or to the Queen to feed her and wash her and collect any new eggs she had laid; or to the Princess to groom her growing wings. Such a scurrying and hurrying and whispering! Mona wondered where Barbara was and how she spent her time. Would she be out on her third-day trail? And where were Uncle Pogo and Nigel?

Just then Barbara came hurrying into Mona's room. "Aunt Phyllis told me she'd bandaged your scent-cone. That means you have to stay in bed today." She looked over her shoulder. "Nigel, come and meet Mona."

Nigel came to the door. He was larger than Mona or Phyllis, with short black hair and strong legs and *ant*ennae that were obviously in perfect receiving and transmitting condition. He was young, and seemed shy.

"What do you work at? Mona asked.

"Oh just around," Nigel said casually. "I'm giving Uncle Pogo a hand with his carrying business. I've not been out of the nest more than a week."

Mona felt so happy and comfortable sitting up in bed against the pillow with her bandaged antenna flopped lightly on the sunflower-petal coverlet and Barbara and Nigel standing as if entranced by their new relative.

"Are you really going to marry a Princess?" Mona asked.

Nigel blushed. "On the second-next Swarm Day. I'm too young for this coming Swarm Day."

"I've never seen a Swarm," Mona said in a happy satisfied way.

"None of us have either," Barbara told her.

"Pero who works with Uncle George in the bakery has seen one. He knows everything about it," Nigel said.

"That's not true," Barbara said. "He's my age and he hasn't seen a Swarm yet."

Why did she sound angry, Mona wondered.

Just then the door of the bedroom opened and in came an untidy-looking ant dressed in black dungarees with a cap set jauntily on the side of his head. A fat fried spider-leg protruded from his mouth; he was hastily finishing his breakfast.

"Gossip gossip gossip. So this is the new member of the family."

Uncle Pogo, Mona thought, liking him inst*ant*ly.

"Uncle Pogo," Barbara and Nigel said together, "This is Mona. . . Mona . . ."

"Mona Minim," Mona said, suddenly shy. "I've got a sore scent-cone."

"A sore scent-cone? Fond*ant* for you twice a day until it's better."

Feeling that this might sound too privileged for a stranger, Mona said hastily, "I'm getting up tomorrow. I'll be able to work then."

"Work work," Uncle Pogo exclaimed disgustedly. "All everyone here thinks of is work work. Except us."

He glanced slyly at Nigel.

"Nigel and I are the only wise members of this family. The female ants are all alike—there's Aunt Phyllis out soldiering, young Barbara here studying and nursing, goodness knows what she'll turn out to be."

He glanced at Barbara as he said this and she gave him an embarrassed smile that Mona could not quite understand.

"Yes, Nigel and I manage very well in the carrying business. A little of this and a little of that. One or two loads a day. Nothing to strain our mandibles or break our *ant*ennae or forelegs. Just a little steady work and plenty of steady rest. On your first day up, if you would like it, Mona Minim, you can come with us."

Feeling rather timid Mona said, "I've only been one—no, two days out of the nest."

She hoped Uncle Pogo would reply, Dear me, only two days out of the nest. Then you must have a little more experience before you come to work.

At first she felt disappointed when he said, "The sooner you come to work the better," and then she knew that he was right, and suddenly she felt tired of just lying in bed with a bandaged scent-cone and the taste of two spider sandwiches with the crusts cut off lingering in her mouth—but they had been delicious sandwiches!

"I'll be up tomorrow," she said cheerfully.

Barbara was anxious to get to her work. "I must go. I have to spend the morning supervising the youngest ants. The games they play and the tricks they get up to! And then I'll be helping Uncle Pogo and Nigel, if it's sunny. We're bringing in the winter food."

And very soon Barbara was gone, and Uncle Pogo and cousin Nigel; and Mona was left lying languidly in bed listening to all the work sounds in the corridors. Presently as she was drowsing and listening and drowsing the door opened and Aunty Reepy, a fat honey-full ant, came in with Mona's fond*ant*.

"This will make you better," she said.

Mona noticed that Aunty Reepy was blind, like Aunt Theodora And thinking of Aunt Theodora she was beginning to feel homesick again when Uncle Pogo returned.

"Honey-break," he said. "Story-time."

"I'm not used to stories," Mona began. "Where I come from . . ."

Then Uncle Pogo began, and when he was talking he didn't seem any more like an untidy-looking ant in rumpled black dungarees, a nuisance ant whom others seemed to think of as good-for-nothing. He was as full of stories as the honey-pot ants are full of honey.

But chiefly Mona remembered one story that he told.

Can you guess what it was?

Well.

It began while Mona listened in breathless amazement. "Once upon a time, not long ago, almost now, there was a little House Ant called Mona Minim. On her first day out of the nest . . ."

"But that's me!" Mona cried.

Her interruption did not stop Uncle Pogo. He went on talking and telling every part of the story, ending, "And there she sat like a Queen drinking honey from a tiny cup and eating spider sandwiches with the crusts cut off."

When he had finished his story Mona did not ask him how he knew but she wondered, and in answer to her unspoken question Uncle Pogo said, trying to sound modest but actually feeling deservedly proud, "I suppose I am clairvoy*ant*."

"What does that mean?"

"It's a gift that some ants, only a few, possess, where they are able to see clearly without being told, into events and ants; like looking into a raindrop and seeing right to the bottom."

Uncle Pogo waved his long *ant*ennae, almost upsetting the tiny plate of half-eaten fond*ant* and the covered jug of nectar.

"You're a perfect companion for Barbara and Nigel, and we're going to let you stay and be in our family. And you can share work and rest and picnics in the Sunflower Forest; and Swarm Days. I hereby welcome you to the Garden Ants. We are very toler*ant* here.

Mona smiled because she guessed she was expected to smile. Then she and Uncle Pogo, the best of friends, sat eating fond*ant* and making ant-jokes and being, as Uncle Pogo described it, "const*ant*ly flipp*ant*, exuber*ant* and f*ant*astic."

Such words, he told Mona, were ant-words, first among the ants and later borrowed by people who did not have the sense to realize the source of their borrowings.

Aunt Phyllis waited until evening to take the bandage off the scent-cone. The inflammation was gone; the cone was healed.

"That's the goodness in the fond*ant*," Aunt Phyllis said wisely as she kissed Mona goodnight. "You can go with Uncle Pogo tomorrow and he might even let you wheel the rubbish cart!"

6. Winter

*D*ays of sun. Lazing and working; helping to push the rubbish cart or being carried in it and tipped out by Nigel; sliding on the sunflower petals during rest-time in the Sunflower Forest and staining clothes that soaked all week in the new whirlaway sycamore gum-nut washtub without the stains coming out; sneaking in to drink the aphids' milk when Uncle Rufus the herdsman, who was also the schoolteacher, was away or off guard; attending a meeting of the Chewing Society and giggling so much and behaving so badly (did Nigel and Barbara and Mona really need to play that game of flicking pieces of leaf at the blind supervisor?) that another visit was forbidden until next spring—"When you young ants will no longer be miscre*ants*," one of the elderly members of the Chewing Society told Mona mysteriously. Working. Lazing. Playing.

And then the dark weather with half the sunlight drained from the sky in a shock of storms and wild winds, and the fallen sunflower petals piled so deep that warning notices marked "Import*ant*: Sunflower Drifts" were put up on the outskirts of the forest. Then the urgent last-minute gathering of flowerpetals and red leaves for winter fires and light and blankets:

nasturtium, geranium, snapdragon, dahlia petals. For some reason this task was always left too late, and this year the supply was scarce as many of the colors had faded, burned in their own self-consuming fires.

And then the long winter hours spent inside the nest. Going to school and cramming and beginning to compile the *ant*hology that is part of every ant's education, with wise sayings, hints and helpful advice; being taken on lecture tours of the nest—the Underground Gardens with their sour-smelling fungi, the store rooms packed with seeds, honey, beetle, spider, earwig, woodlouse preserves neat in their small labeled jars; the fuel room —a dazzling glory of vermilion, yellow, orange, gold and red; the larvae chamber. Listening and trying to take notes on Sociology, Monarchy, Anatomy, Scent-Cone Care, Duties of Public and Private Stomachs.

Mona and Nigel and Barbara grew weary of learning, and bored with tours of the nest and note-taking, and sometimes showing their boredom too clearly they were punished. There was the frightening time when Nigel blocked all his scent-cones to see what would happen. He had to be rushed to hospital and nursed day and night and for a while it appeared as if he would have such a long period of convalescence that he would miss his first Swarm Day, but as he was a healthy young ant he recovered at last.

"It was only to see what would happen," he kept protesting.

"Well you learned your lesson," Aunt Phyllis said, sternly clopping her jaws up and down.

From time to time Mona felt afraid of Aunt Phyllis and her stern soldierly bearing but as she became accustomed to being among the Garden Ants she grew used to having a soldier for an aunt and her life among her own species seemed so dist*ant* that she wondered if she had dreamed it. Where was Aunt Theodora? Perhaps she was dead, she had been so old. And where was Pamela? Perhaps she too was spending the winter in furthering her education, but being a House Ant she would have more luxuries to enjoy and more dangers to face.

"You have to be very cunning to be a House Ant," Mona told the eagerly listening younger ants when it was her turn to supervise at story hour and they had pleaded, as they always did, for a 'story about the House Ants.'

"You have to be alert. Here when you go in search of honey you know it's honey when you find it because it smells and tastes like honey and what can a young ant trust if she cannot trust her senses that are sharper than the sharpest eye of the eagle that lives miles and miles up the mountainside and is able to see a spider, a snail—an ant!—from such a height."

One by one the little ants looked up at the roof of the recreation room as if they expected an eagle to come plunging through to seize them.

"Oh yes, among the Garden Ants you can believe your sharpest senses. But there, among the House Ants, the people put out china pools of sweetest honey-smelling and honey-tasting liquid and you go down to the edge of the pool and you sit by it, just like sitting down beside a sweet raindrop that has spread everywhere; and you dip your foot in, thinking, I'm going to swim in honey. What a luxury to be a House Ant!

"And then it happens."

The little ants were *ant*ennae-trembling with *ant*icipation.

"What happens?"

Mona looked at them in a superior manner. "You're poisoned, dead," she said sharply.

"Oh-Oh-Oh-Oh." The black eyes gazing at her were big and round and serious.

"Poisoned, dead," she repeated, for effect.

The little ants shivered with excitement.

Mona told them other stories too. How the House Ants were able to obtain more delicacies for parties and feasts. How their clothes were the height of fashion, *haute couture*, sewn from remn*ant*s.

"Remn*ant*s are pieces of unwanted silks and satins and nylons which the people leave out for the ants to take home."

There were so many stories to tell about the House Ants and Mona found she had forgotten so much that she used to invent many of the stories and after she had invented them and the little ants asked, wonderingly, "Is that really true?"

Mona said, "Yes, it's true," because it seemed to be true and then it *was* true.

"They were Great Days among the House Ants," Mona said impressively.

And so the winter days passed. Mona received Honors in her first Sense-Recognition-Communication Examination and was given a tiny ant's tear-drop pend*ant* on a spun silver chain. And Barbara, finishing her second examination was given a book, *Tales of EnchANTment for Young Female Ants*. And although Nigel did not get high marks in his examination, as he'd been convalescent and he was more interested, too, in other things than in being a scholar, he was given a special book called *Adventures in ANTwerp*, the story of a young male ant who recklessly defied International Fumigation Laws by living in the kitchen of a jet aircraft.

At night Barbara and Nigel sat in the sitting room on the *ant*ique chairs, leaning against the spider-lace *ant*imacassars and read their books aloud to Mona. And just when they had finished reading and were beginning to get restless again, and they might have forgotten about being good and Nigel might have been driven through sheer boredom to try some more disastrous trick than that of the blocked scent-cones, it was announced that the young Princess who was to be Queen on the next Swarm Day was to be named and honored at a special feast to which all the members of the colony were invited.

At once preparations were made for the Feast.

7. By the Geranium Fire

"Yes," Aunt Phyllis said, "you may go tomorrow to the Feast if you are good."

As Mona lay in bed that evening she saw in her mind the beautiful young Princess and the wedding dress that was being flown by jet from South America under the care of the cousin of the cousin of Uncle Rufus who had emigrated from Peru and had studied to be a tailor. In her imagination Mona tasted the delights of the honey-feasting and savored the early spring air on the first day out of the nest after a long winter. The hours passed and she found she could not sleep for excitement. She wondered if Barbara were awake. She climbed out of bed and crept along the corridor to Barbara's room.

At Barbara's door she stopped.

"Barbara."

She pushed open the door.

"Are you awake?"

"Yes," Barbara said. "I was wondering if you were awake."

Mona thought she had been crying. But how could that be? Nothing sad had happened.

"Why are you sad, Barbara?"

And then as they sat by the geranium fire Barbara told Mona the story of her life, how when she was born it was summertime and food was plentiful and the sun was shining every day and all the ants born in that season were big and strong and grew quickly and many were now training to be soldiers but Barbara didn't think she would be a soldier; she hadn't decided what she wanted to be. And she told Mona how one day while she was playing in the *ant*eroom to the nursery one of the older ants who was her nursemaid for the day said, jokingly,

"What are those bumps on your back, Barbara? Don't tell me you're growing wings!"

Some other ant heard and the news spread and soon Barbara was surrounded by ants clamoring to inspect her wings. And when Aunt Phyllis came to take Barbara home someone said loudly, "Barbara's growing wings."

"You can imagine how I felt," Barbara said gloomily. "I knew I wasn't growing wings. You can't believe how everybody behaved. And though I knew I wasn't growing wings, well, you know how you begin to wonder if something's going to happen when everyone seems to believe it will happen. Wings!"

Mona's black eyes were shining.

"Wings," she breathed. "You would fly up in the sky and smell the sun and everything and look down on the earth. I wonder what is the smell of being up in the sky?"

She stopped in her dreaming. She did not think Barbara had heard her. Barbara was gazing into the geranium fire. One geranium petal was guaranteed to last for days burning its light and warmth but this was already fading with a gray stain spreading from the edges to the center of the petal.

"Aunt Phyllis will be angry. We've burned half a geranium petal," Barbara said, poking at the curling gray edges with a polished strip of beetle-back, the chief substance, next to snail-shell and woodlouse armor, used in ant furniture and furnishings.

Barbara resumed her story. "There was all this talk of having a Princess in the family. The doctor examined me and said I might be a late-developing Princess like one of Uncle Rufus's cousins, the South American red ant he's always talking about."

Mona had heard the story.

"I remember I used to twist and turn, trying to see my wings in the mirror. But I knew I didn't have wings. I just didn't feel like a Princess either."

"Wouldn't you like to be one?"

"Oh yes, but it's the way you're made. I knew I wouldn't grow up to be a Queen."

"What happened then?" Mona looked sympathetic as Barbara's eyes filled with tears.

"Every time anyone came to visit Aunt Phyllis would say, Come here Barbara and show us your wings. How proud she was! Of course she herself is big and strong, big enough to have been a Queen. And when she found I wasn't growing wings she was far more disappointed than I. It seems that I could have grown wings if people wanted me to be a Princess and as you know, in our world an ant can do whatever she wants to do as long as the other members of the colony want it too. But we already had a Princess! And there was Aunt Phyllis going on and on . . . . I wouldn't want to be a young ant again would you, Mona Minim?"

Mona thought. "I don't know. I don't really remember. I'm glad I'm not a Queen though. I would be bored to death just laying eggs and everyone fussing around me. Why, our Big Queen's so big she can hardly move. They say she has enough eggs to last her until she dies and she'll still be laying eggs when we're bossy old members of the Chewing Society."

They laughed then. Mona made a chopping movement with her mandibles. "Chew chew chew, chew chew chew."

"But it will be fun to go to the Naming and the Feast, won't it? And the glowworms are bringing fireworks. And there'll be a big geranium, nasturtium and dahlia fire. That's why Aunt Phyllis will be angry with us for burning half a petal."

"And George the baker is going to do tricks."

But Barbara had fallen into a dream again. "If I had grown wings," she began, "and if I had been a Queen I wonder how it would feel? Just think what it must be like to fly!"

"You can fly without wings. Remember *Adventures in ANTwerp?* And then the cousin of the cousin of Uncle Rufus who brought the wedding dress all the way from South America by jet?"

So Barbara and Mona sat by the geranium fire talking of Princesses and Queens and wings and flying until the geranium petal burned lower and lower and became embers that glowed faintly and then died. The geranium fire was in ashes.

Mona shivered. "I'm cold."

Barbara shivered. "And it's past midnight."

Mona yawned.

Barbara yawned.

Mona yawned again, this time remembering to put her *ant*ennae politely over her mouth.

Barbara yawned again and her head began to nod.

And both ants with just enough wakefulness to last until they climbed into their beds, said goodnight, and Mona tiptoed from the room leaving Barbara already half-asleep.

Mona crept along the corridor. All was quiet save the tick-ticking of the clock beetle. Mona listened. Past midnight. She could see a glowworm light in the nursery on the lower floor. An ant was being born, perhaps. Or the Big Queen had awakened and was restless and calling for her maid. But there was no sound of any ant moving. A soft whispering came from the grass as it grew; it was a business-like whispering, arguments among different grassblades about which path to take to the sky, decisions when the argument had been settled, then the whispering quietness as the steady work of growth continued. There was a knock-knocking from one or two late-wandering earthworms, and shiftings and grindings and sometimes a roaring sound as particles of earth settled and turned in their sleep and the blind roots of trees and shrubs and flowers twitched in their dreaming or unclenched a fist to grasp the earth more securely.

Mona listened. She could smell darkness and rain. In the past season the glowworms had been scarce, having migrated south to the limestone caves. The corridor was not well lit. Mona's shadow crept along beside her and she shivered and she might have grown afraid had she not at last reached the door of her bedroom. Uncle Pogo and Aunt Phyllis and Nigel and Barbara were all in bed asleep.

I'm the only one in the family awake, Mona thought. A feeling of loneliness came over her as she remembered her real family, the House Ants. Aunt Phyllis and Uncle Pogo and Barbara and Nigel were a wonderful family to be adopted into but Mona couldn't help remembering, not often, but at times suddenly and vividly the smells of the House-Ant nest; the wood and the iron and steel of the cupboard beneath the sink; the constant perils of floods as water flowed unpredictably down the iron pipes through the hole in the floor where the House Ants lived, down the side of the garage to—where? Mona had never found out. At night she had fallen asleep to the sound of water flowing and gurgling in the drainpipes.

Perhaps some day when she was bigger and stronger and older she would put all her possessions in a handkerchief, say goodbye to Aunt Phyllis and Uncle Pogo and Nigel and Barbara, and set out on the journey home.

Some Day.

Not yet.

Some Day.

And in the meantime, tomorrow, she was going to be allowed to attend the naming of the Princess.

She slept. She dreamed that Aunt Theodora appeared in the distance beyond hills of golden honey, but Aunt Theodora did not seem to notice the honey. Mona could hear her voice clearly: "Little Mona Minim, come home to the House Ants. Have you forgotten the life among the House Ants? Aunt Theodora, Pamela, the Stair Game that you never played, the snug nest in the beam of the garage roof? Come home, Mona Minim!"

In her sleep Mona became frightened. "I'm too small," she pleaded. "I don't know the way and I might get lost in the Sunflower Forest."

"Lost in the Sunflower Forest indeed," a voice said, and opening her eyes Mona saw that it was morning and Aunt Phyllis was already dressed in her soldier uniform ready for work.

"Time to get up," she said. "You'd better not be lost in the Sunflower Forest. We're holding the Naming of the Princess near the Forest. We need every available *ant*enna and mandible and plain honest ant-leg to help carry the provisions for the feast."

8. Naming Day

and a Disaster

*I*t was cold above the earth. There was little sun or sign of spring. Mona, at the end of her third journey, rested against the withered stems of the sunflower plants. Why can't we have the feast when the sun is out? she thought. She kept remembering her dream and thinking about the House Ants, and she was frowning when Uncle Pogo arrived with his cartload of food.

"Little Mona Minim, you will turn into a worrying ant. What's the matter?"

"I'm afraid. I don't know why," Mona said.

Uncle Pogo looked serious. "So you have caught it too?"

"Caught what?"

"Something in the air. As a clairvoy*ant* I feel it. Say nothing to the others."

"But what is it, Uncle Pogo?"

Uncle Pogo sighed. "I don't know. I don't know, little Mona Minim. Perhaps your fear is only natural. Every ant is afraid after being in the nest most of the winter. We have to relearn and remember our trails. Some of the big-heads never get past the entrance to the nest, they're so timid. They just stand and think, Tomorrow I'll make it, tomorrow, tomorrow.

But tomorrow never comes. They're useful as sentries though, because their big heads block the entrance to the nest. But you're Mona Minim, a brave little ant."

"I'm not brave," Mona said. "Why do you say I'm brave, Uncle Pogo?"

Uncle Pogo turned away to continue his work. "You may need to be brave, Mona."

Then Mona forgot her fears in helping Uncle Pogo to carry the loaves of bread and the honey-rolls and the spider-wing crisps out to the picnic ground at the edge of the Forest.

And then it happened.

When?

At three o'clock in the afternoon.

What happened?

Who can say exactly what happened? How can you tell afterward what exactly happened when it is all so sudden and terrifying?

Three o'clock.

The trestle tables set ready in the middle of the picnic ground. Then a rush of air and sound came out of the sky and only Mona recognized the sound as a human voice which cried, "This one!"

Or, "This is it!"

Or, "Got it!"

It was the eleven-year-old Peter who lived in the House.

Then a huge building with glass walls descended from the wintry sky upon a small group of ants by the table nearest the Forest, and before any ant had time to think what was happening a swift stroke of the child's hand had captured several and swept them into the glass building. Feeling the rush of draft from the descending hand Mona struggled as if caught in a hurricane. She tripped and fell, lay still recovering her wits, then crawled through the grass, and looking up, saw the glass building and the child's hand ascending and through the glass walls two tiny black *ant*ennae struggling and waving and pressed against the glass, magnified and strange in the gray winter light—Barbara's frightened face. Mona had no time to recognize any of the other prisoners before the glass building and the child who carried and controlled it had disappeared.

After a while the shaking earth was still. The flattened grass sprang shaking to its roots, wiping away the human footprints. Tables had been overturned. The remaining members of the ant colony, scurrying and hurrying wildly in all directions could not seem to decide what to do. In the general panic some attacked members of their own family. Mona watched in horror, unable to move or help, as George the baker, a kind ant, a great favorite with the young ones, attacked and killed Pero his only nephew and then proceeded to drag the body carefully toward the colony cemetery, as if he did not know it was his only nephew he had killed: Pero who lived in his house and shared the baking duties.

Other ants rushed up to the fat feeding ants who had arranged themselves as feeding-posts for the workers, and then as if the prospect were one of famine and not of capture and imprisonment, they began to pump the poor ants dry of honey. Old-maid ants ran in frantic circles trying to feed the bewildered young ones who were suddenly the object of their tender care.

And then, in a flash, every ant knew exactly what to do. The trails were established as if nothing had happened. The scent of home trembled in each hair of *ant*ennae. Feeling herself calm now and very much a part of the colony Mona began to help with the loaves of bread that had fallen from the trestle-tables and taking a loaf in her jaws she followed the long orderly line that had begun to move toward the nest, walking on and on without stumbling although her legs were tired and the shock had weakened her so much that she longed to lie down in the grass and rest. Uncle Pogo, behind her, made jokes.

"We did not *ant*icipate this," he said.

With her newly found energy and sympathy with the colony Mona found that she could smile even at Uncle Pogo's untimely joking.

Later at a hurried meeting to count the remaining ants and try to discover the fate of those missing, Mona realized that she, as a House Ant, had the advantage of superior education in human affairs, and while the others listened she explained:

"It was the boy Peter who lives in the House. He has an Ant Farm. An Ant Farm is a house made especially for ants who are captured and forced to live in it."

A small piping voice came, "Forever?"

"Until they die. Or escape."

"Has any ant ever escaped?"

"I've heard of it though I've not known it personally. Some of our colony were taken just before I was born and I used to hear about it when I was little. Uncles and Aunts used to talk of those who were captured for the Ant Farm, and then they would turn to me and say, 'Before you were born, Mona Minim.' "

"How did this child, Peter, get such a . . . weapon?"

"His mother gave it to him, I believe, for his birthday. The people," Mona explained, "are not like us. Where we have just one Big Queen for a mother and our father is lost or dead or something, the people have a mother and father each, usually, though sometimes it gets mixed up. And when the people come out of their eggs they are given presents and afterward on their hatching day they are given a present. The people are strange," Mona mused. "They have stolen much of our language. If only you could hear them, the way they talk about us all the time!

A loud voice called. "What we want to know, Mona Minim, is this: Is there any hope of escape for our loved ones?"

"I don't know," Mona said, suddenly wanting to cry, and remembering Barbara's frightened face pressed against the window.

"But you must know. You're a House Ant. You've lived among the people."

Mona began to cry. "I don't know," she sobbed. "Unless, unless someone tries to rescue them."

They were all looking at her. She heard someone say, "She's a House Ant. She ought to know how to go about it."

Grateful, she heard Uncle Pogo's reply. "Nonsense. Mona Minim is too small and young. She's but a baby."

"All the same she's a House Ant."

"What's she doing among us, I'd like to know!"

"Whose smell has she stolen?"

"Why doesn't she volunteer to rescue the captured members of the colony if she knows so much about it?"

Mona felt everlastingly grateful to Uncle Pogo for waving his *ant*ennae fiercely to command silence.

"Stop this nonsense, every one of you. You can see the young ant is bewildered. Leave her. Don't forget we still have to hold the ceremony of naming the Princess. The life of the colony must go on. We'll have the ceremony inside the Assembly Hall. And we'll have to make a record of the missing ants. My niece Barbara was one of those captured. And later we'll decide about plans for rescue."

Uncle Pogo stopped speaking as suddenly as he had started. He seemed surprised at having spoken at all. Aunt Phyllis who had come in late from field operations was standing at the back of the room looking very proud, but when she tried to make a sign to Uncle Pogo to continue his unexpected public speaking he did not respond. One of the stout milit*ant* females got up to speak in a loud voice and someone began to question her about Mona Minim.

Gently Uncle Pogo led Mona from the room. Aunt Phyllis and Nigel followed. Nigel appeared to be in a state of shock; he did not speak. Mona wondered if he had witnessed the killing of Pero.

"I shan't go to the naming," Mona said.

"You stay by the fire with me," Uncle Pogo said.

So that evening while Aunt Phyllis and Nigel went to the Assembly Hall for the naming ceremony Mona and Uncle Pogo sat by the geranium fire and Uncle Pogo told Mona a story.

"Once, not long ago, almost now, there was a little House Ant called Mona Minim. On her first day out of the nest she was lost, and she made a friend called Barbara, a Garden Ant, who found her and took her home to live and gave her food and let her stay in bed eating spider sandwiches with the crusts cut off until her scent-cone was healed."

"Why, that's me," Mona cried.

"And then another day, the day of the Naming of the Princess, Barbara and some of her friends were captured and taken to an Ant Farm."

"Why that's us!" Mona exclaimed.

"And then another day when little Mona Minim felt bigger and stronger and wanted to return home to the House Ants and to rescue Barbara, she put all her possessions in a ladybird handkerchief and set out on her journey."

This time Mona did not say, Why, that's me. Instead, she kept silent and looked thoughtfully into the geranium fire. But she knew Uncle Pogo meant her, and Uncle Pogo must have known she knew for he said,

"Even a little ant like Mona Minim can be brave. One day, Mona Minim, one day not too far ahead, one day in springtime..."

But Mona did not hear any more. She had fallen asleep and she slept right through evening and all night and she did not even hear Aunt Phyllis and Nigel come home from Princess Antonia's party.

9. *"You Are Not Chewing Hard Enough, Mona Minim"*

*T*he days that followed were gloomy. The promised spring was late, a rainstorm came and washed away one of the upper tunnels and the water leaked through to the nest chamber rising halfway to the ceiling, drowning a number of young ants. Because the colony was diminished in strength there were not enough workers to take the boats (fragments of snail-shell) into the flooded tunnels to rescue the marooned ants, and some of these were drowned. It was urgent that the eggs should be taken into the sun to be dried and inspected, but how could they be if there was no sign of the sun? Each ant in the colony was now doing almost twice its work. Even Uncle Pogo and Nigel and other male ants who by tradition were reluctant workers were taking extra loads of food and clothing while Nigel worked during meal-hours in the Underground Gardens, making channels for the raindrops in a hastily improvised system of drainage. Ants that had seldom been heard of during the smooth operation of the colony suddenly became public figures with ideas and plans to propose. George the baker, after a period of mourning for his nephew whose death he seemed not to remember, became the new leader of the Excitement Center. Mona had never mentioned Pero's death to Nigel and Nigel never mentioned it to her, though sometimes Mona remembered it and relived the afternoon of horror. George became absorbed in his work. He would lie in wait for passing ants, approach them, and urgently communicate his ideas. The ideas spread. The colony found itself with a new excitement and purpose. What did it matter if each evening every ant fell asleep exhausted and yet was forced to get up early the following morning for work?

Yet this eagerness to restore harmony and prosperity could not alone dry the eggs that had lain for so long in the damp nursery chambers. The colony depended most of all on its eggs for the emerging young ants who with good food and sunlight would grow strong enough to be soldiers and workers.

If only the sun would shine! If only the promised spring and the warm days would come!

Now although Mona was a House Ant and although members of the colony now kept reminding her of her House Ant-ness, as she reminded herself often enough in her dreaming, she worked as hard as the others carrying double loads with Uncle Pogo and yet managing to play boats with Nigel in the little boat that had been built for three and where, now, Barbara's empty seat and the memories it held served to make the boating expeditions mournful affairs. Where is Barbara now? Mona and Nigel would wonder. What is she doing? Are they kind to her? Has she enough to eat?

It was one afternoon when Mona was at a meeting of the Chewing Society that she realized that the members of the colony had not forgotten what they had been thinking and feeling and talking about on the night of the Naming Day.

"You're not chewing hard enough, Mona Minim," her neighbor, Edith Ant, remarked as Mona chewed on her share of beetle's body, making it to a pulp to feed the young ants.

Mona felt annoyed. "I *am* chewing hard enough Edith Ant."

Edith stopped chewing. "House Ant," she whispered fiercely, as if it were an insult.

"Garden Ant," Mona retorted equally fiercely.

Aunt Fortuna, who was the blind supervisor of the Chewing Society and had once worked as a soldier but was now a gentle ant, half-nursemaid half babysitter and guardian, spoke quietly, "Mona and Edith, get on with your chewing."

Mona and Edith took up their portion of beetle's body but though they seemed very busy Edith was able to whisper again, "House Ant!"

And Mona was able to reply, "Garden Ant!"

The older ants near Edith heard her and said nothing. One, a member of George's family, who had made herself a smart new outfit of clothes now that George was a public figure and members of his family might be called upon to appear in society, whispered sympathetically to Mona, "Are you really going to do it?"

"Do what?" Mona asked.

She was tired and irritable with so much working. "Do what?" she repeated crossly, not at all like the goodmannered little ant she used to be.

"What they're planning for you."

"What are they planning?"

"Don't you know? Hasn't your Aunt or Uncle told you? All day George has been at the Excitement Center suggesting that because you are a House Ant with knowledge of Ant Farms you should find some way to free the imprisoned members of the colony."

"But I'm only little," Mona pleaded. "When you're little you don't rescue. Other ants rescue for you."

"Well," said the older ant. "You know that what the leader of the Excitement Center suggests must be carried out. George Ant is very good at exciting. I saw him shake one of the old honey-pots until the poor ant could hardly restrain herself from coming at once to tell you not only of your obligation to rescue the imprisoned ants but..."

"But what?"

"But—I don't say this is my personal opinion, mind you—I mean..."

The ant was confused and embarrassed. "You should go home to your House Ants. Perhaps if you had never come here all this would never have happened." She waved her *ant*ennae vaguely around as she said "All this."

"All what?"

Mona was aware that other members of the Chewing Society were staring at her. All seemed so much older and wiser than she. If only Barbara were there to help her and speak up for her! Barbara or Uncle Pogo or someone. Just to say that she was too small to rescue the imprisoned ants, that she didn't know where to look or which trail to take, that she'd be lost and afraid all by herself in the Sunflower Forest.

And yet while she was thinking these thoughts and being afraid, she knew what the answer would be if she protested. She knew that no ant is really too small to work or to rescue, and that whether you are born a Garden Ant or a House Ant you know this just as you know whether you'll be a Princess and future Queen or if you'll have a chance to be the mother of a Prince. You just know because you're an ant and it's an ant's way to know, and it's as plain as your scent, and once you've passed your first Sense-Recognition-Communication Examination you've no excuse, certainly not the excuse of being too small.

How far away, to Mona, seemed her first eventful day out of the nest, her infantile dream of playing the Stair Game, her accident, her rescue, and then the first day among the Garden Ants when she sat up in bed drinking warm nectar and eating spider sandwiches with the crusts cut off while Uncle Pogo told his stories!

That evening before Mona went to bed she found a spotted ladybird handkerchief that had been left behind by a visiting ladybird. I will put my possessions in this, she thought. And on the first sunny day, which might also be Swarm Day, I shall set out on my journey home and I will find Barbara as I promised I would find her if ever she became lost, and I will rescue her.

It is easy, isn't it, to be brave when you are tucked up warm in your little ant-bed?

10. "Do You Carry Two Lawn Handkerchiefs, Mona Minim?"

The next day was sunny. But did Mona take her possessions and wrapping them in her ladybird handkerchief set out on her journey? Oh no.

"I'll wait a while longer until the earth and the grass are dry and I'll be able to sleep out at night without being drowned in dewdrops, for as I'm such a small ant I shan't be able to carry extras like bedding, not if I'm also going to take my antennae brush and a change of clothing and my six red resting-slippers and my sunbonnet. . . .

The more things Mona thought of to take on her journey the more each one seemed necessary. She would need to borrow Uncle Pogo's rubbish cart if she were to take everything she believed she needed.

The sunny day sent every ant into a dizzying hurry of delight and work. The scouts returned from a morning's exploration to report that if the fine weather continued and the air was still damp, but not cold, Swarm Day could be held within a week. They'd selected a Viewing Spot, a huge mound that would hold most of the colony. If they'd not lost several members of the colony to the Ant Farm they would have sought, they said, a larger mound;

but this was just right. Every ant would have a clear view. The young Princess would have a convenient rise to begin her flight and not put too much strain at first on her untried wings. And the young males, too, would have a fair chance in their race to marry the Princess. The scouts were sure that after this Swarm Day at least there'd be no complaining about blocked views or wailings from the youngest ants that they couldn't see what was going on and no one bothered to clear a space for them; or the more serious charges from some of the disappointed males that there'd been no room for them to take off, and that the space had been arranged beforehand, unfairly, through family influence or bribery.

Uncle Rufus whose cousin's cousin had arrived with the wedding dress by jet was most helpful. He set up an Information Center just inside the nest from where he distributed leaflets, Aeronautics for Young Ants, A Guide For Swarm Day Particip*ants. Ant*idotes for Flying Sickness. Import*ant* Hints for Young Gall*ants*. There was also an interesting pamphlet which was withdrawn because it was thought to be too revolutionary, "The Jet Age. Are Wings Outmoded?"

Mona felt the feverish excitement that swept the colony. The air was full of secrets and promises. If only Barbara had been there to share it!

Mona had decided that on Swarm Day when every ant was so busy that unusual activities would not be noticed she would set out on her journey home. The rescue of Barbara seemed a formidable task. She planned to succeed in it, to invite the rescued ants to stay for a while in the House Ant nest and then with promises and invitations to visit and spend holidays and workdays Mona would stand, a heroine, at the entrance to the House Ant Nest, waving farewell to an eternally grateful Barbara who would turn to wave, clutching the little pot of real raspberry jam that Mona had made for her, and then Barbara and the other rescued members of the colony would follow their trail toward the Sunflower Forest.

What dreams! How can you make such dreams come true if you can't even decide whether to take your sunbonnet and your six red resting-slippers? or your best or your second-best *ant*ennae brush? Mona's best brush was made of finest thistledown with a back of real gold that Nigel had found on one of the tunnels and Uncle Pogo had polished—it was about the size of a large sunbeam, and as full of light and mirror-reflections. Oh it was hard to decide whether to take it and risk losing it or leave it and perhaps never see it again! Aunt Phyllis was too busy soldiering to bother with a little ant who asked foolishly:

"Please, Aunt Phyllis, if you were going on a long long journey and had to choose between taking your best or your second-best *ant*ennae brush, which would you choose?"

Even Uncle Pogo, helping to distribute the leaflets for Swarm Day, was too busy to listen. As for Nigel—he spent all his time now with the other young males who were swarming on the second-next Swarm Day and who were now following the older male ants everywhere, giving them the devoted attention accorded to heroes.

Mona was forced to make her plans alone. She'd never made plans before but she had an idea that in making a plan you found a sheet of leaf-paper and took your spider-leg pencil (if Uncle Pogo hadn't eaten it—he was always eating spider-leg pencils, even those preserved in formic acid which were no good for eating. After eating these Uncle Pogo usually had to take a spoonful of *Ant*acid Powder that he kept in a jar on a shelf of the store room.)

Yes. Making plans you found your paper, took your spider-leg pencil, drew a diagram with arrows and signs. You made a pencil trail to help you. You wrote numbered instructions to yourself in a neat list. Then when your plan was complete you folded it in four folds and put it in your pocket and during your journey you took your plan from your pocket, unfolded it, and consulted it.

But what if all that would fit into your pocket was your white lawn handkerchief?

Feeling very bold Mona went to the cousin of the cousin of Uncle Rufus. "If you have a spare moment," she requested in her most polite voice, "Would you be so kind as to sew another pocket in my red velvet dress?"

The cousin of the cousin of Uncle Rufus who was wishing he were back in South America and who was feeling irritable because he had stayed up all night to make alterations to Princess Antonia's wedding dress, asked abruptly, "Why do you want another pocket when you already have one? Do you carry *two* lawn handkerchiefs, Mona Minim?"

"No," said Mona in a small voice.

"Then you don't need another pocket."

Mona was dismissed. She did not even have a chance to see the wedding dress.

She decided she would carry her plan in her sunbonnet.

11. Swarm Day

and a Departure

*S*warm Day. The excitement spread like a kind of sickness. Even before sunrise there were ants on the mound, waiting, having seized the best vantage points. Princess Antonia's taking-off area was fenced with sunrays that had been gathered the day before and preserved. A notice hung at the entrance: "Princess Antonia and Attendants Only."

The males who were taking part in the Swarm were arriving, and finding their space restricted they'd begun to fight each other for taking-off room.

Feeling sick with the excitement of the Swarm and the disappointment of not being able to witness it, her First Swarm, and then the worry about her secret departure Mona watched as one by one the ants with their picnic baskets and thistledown rugs set out toward the Mound.

"Coming, Mona?" Uncle Pogo called.

Mona excused herself. "Oh. I must go to the nursery to help with the younger ants. Don't wait for me."

"Well be quick, Mona. You don't want to miss your first Swarm. It's a great day for Swarming."

"Oh it is indeed," Mona replied.

From almost every passing ant she heard a similar remark: "A great day for Swarming. We've never had such a, day."

"What a day! Now last year..."

And the older ants searched their memories. "Why, I remember on my first Swarm Day..."

How exciting it was, and sad, and frightening! Only the evening before, Mona had passed their neighbor's quarters where the young male, Wallace, who was taking part in today's Swarm had been creating a disturbance. Mona heard him crying out, "I don't want to, I don't want to fly tomorrow. I'll wait till next Swarm Day. Please don't ask me to fly tomorrow."

Why did he seem afraid? Mona's heart beat fast with curiosity and dread. She stayed outside the door long enough to hear Wallace's Aunt and Uncle speaking sharply to him, "You'll do as you were born to do. You'll go swarming tomorrow, my young ant, and no nonsense!"

Why was he so frightened? Mona wondered. And then she remembered

that there were always rumors about Swarm Day, that some of the older ants refused to talk about it, and Mona had always supposed it was because they hadn't been born with wings, they had never flown and did not know the smell of the sky and the sun, and reminding them of what they longed for had made them sad.

But once when as an indiscreet young ant she had asked outright, "Are you unhappy that you never knew the smell of the sun?" she had not been able to understand the answer, "Unhappy? Maybe. But once you know the smell of the sun what hope is there . . ."

The older ant had stopped speaking.

"Run away and work or play, Mona Minim, and don't ask questions."

Now having overheard Wallace and his crying and the fear in his voice Mona remembered her question of long ago and the answer that she could not understand. What does it mean? she wondered.

But now there were too many things to do and no time to stand wondering. Almost every ant except the guardians and nurses had left the nest and Mona, in pretense of helping with the babies, hurried down to the egg chamber. How dim and quiet it was! There was a damp earthy smell. The rows of charges lay still, wrapped tightly in their white blankets. What was the Big Queen doing? Mona wondered. Dare she peep in at her?

Tiptoeing to the *Ante*chamber she peeped into the Queen's room, and was disconcerted when the Big Queen, opening her eyes from sleep, said, "Who are you? What are you doing here?"

She stared at Mona.

"I'm Mona Minim." Mona didn't know what else to say.

"Why aren't you out with the Swarm, Mona Minim?"

"I'm going out later," Mona said. Then very boldly she asked, "Why haven't you gone to see the Swarm, Big Queen?"

The Big Queen sighed and closed her eyes and opened them again. "There's only one Swarm Day in the life of a Queen," she said. "Once in a lifetime, little Mona Minim."

"And you flew?"

"Yes, I flew."

"What's it like up in the air away from the smell of the earth? What is the smell of blue and of the high winds that never come down as far as the grass and the sunflowers? What is the smell of the sun when you're so close to it?"

The Big Queen smiled. "What a curious ant you are. Now off you go to the Swarm, Mona Minim, and see and smell and hear and touch for yourself what it means."

Quietly Mona crept along the corridor to her bedroom. Opening the closet she took her ladybird handkerchief that was well packed with her possessions (including her best *ant*ennae brush) and putting on her sunbonnet with the plan safely inside it she hurried toward the entrance to the nest.

"You're looking very smart," the sentry on duty remarked. "But you'll have to hurry. I think it's begun."

Mona did indeed hurry, first along the trail toward the Swarming Mound where she turned sharply left in the general direction that would be taken by the flying ants; but her trail was now hers alone: she wanted to avoid any members of the colony. She hurried on toward the Sunflower Forest, and because it was really a long way and because her bundle was heavier than she had supposed it would be she stopped at the entrance to the Forest and with not another ant in sight nor, it seemed, any other creature, Mona ·sat down, unfolded her picnic sandwiches, uncorked her bottle of nectar and enjoyed a delicious lunch.

The others will be having lunch too, she thought, with a pang of loneliness.

And the Swarm will have happened.

She tried not to think she was leaving Uncle Pogo and Aunt Phyllis and Nigel forever. Once she had rescued Barbara and the other ants there would be visits, and holidays, wouldn't there?

Settling down for an after-lunch nap, although this was not in her original plan, she thought and dreamed about the events of her life. You couldn't really say goodbye to other ants once you had known them; you would always remember them.

She looked up at the sky. She fancied that she saw, high in the air, close to the sun, a crowd of flying ants, now rising, now falling, now seeming motionless, suspended in air; was it a crowd of flying ants or were they dust or black sunbeams or thunder clouds that had broken to pieces and were falling?

Mona closed her eyes and slept.

12. Queen Antonia

*M*ona woke up. How late it was! And lateness wasn't in the Plan. The plan said, distinctly, Travel Through Sunflower Forest, Reach Barbara's Rest-Bed and Stair-Trail by Sundown. Sleep in Rest-Bed. Find Discarded Clothes. Acquire House-Ant Smell.

Mona felt that she must have been asleep for hours at the edge of the Sunflower Forest. She began to wonder if perhaps she were not being a foolish rather than a brave ant, for she feared what would happen should darkness overtake her in her journey through the Forest. She decided that it might be wiser for her to remain where she was overnight. And then she wished she'd brought her *ant*hology to read. Her personal *ant*hology was small and she could have tucked it inside her sunbonnet, but it was too late now for regrets.

So she sat down and thought and thought. It was a novel situation for her not to be able to rest and not to be able to work but only to be able to try to decide whether to rest or to work. How confusing it was! Especially when a fear of being foolish and a longing to be brave kept interrupting her trail of thought just as an unfamiliar scent might interrupt on a Garden or House Ant trail.

Which? How? Where?

Suddenly she sensed a movement in the grass near her. She heard a moaning sound as if some insect were in a state of great exhaustion, and yet there was no cry for help, and there did not seem to be tears or weeping, only the rustling in the grass and the deep sighs that seemed to be half distress and half joy. Now how could that be? Mona wondered, creeping toward the sound and thinking perhaps it was only an autumn leaf and the rustling of its dying fire. Reaching forward her *ant*ennae Mona parted the stalks of grass and was astonished to see Princess Antonia lying with her wedding dress all crumpled and torn, and her not seeming to care about it at all. Why was she lying there? Was the Swarming over? Why didn't she look radiant like a young Queen? And all that lovely specially woven spider-lace from South America crushed and ruined, and one fragment of the lace torn completely from the beautiful wedding dress—but—why—it wasn't lace, not that beautiful piece. lying in shreds beside Queen Antonia, it was her wing, but it couldn't be—it was not lace, it was her beautiful wing.

"Oh your wing is broken," Mona cried, hurrying forward to help the poor young Queen and understanding now her extreme state of distress.

Queen Antonia stared with dreamy eyes. Surely she was not *happy*, Mona thought.

"Your wing, your beautiful wing!"

Queen Antonia smiled. "I've been trying to rub it off all afternoon," she said. "It's getting dark and I'm exhausted and I must find a dark place in the earth to rest and lay my eggs."

"But what about your wings?"

Queen Antonia did not answer except to say, "Will you pull the other wing off for me, Mona?"

Mona was horrified. "Pull your wing off? Your wing that took you up in the sky and you smelled the color of blue and of the wind that stays so high it never comes near the earth and the grass and the sunflowers? Is there grass in the sky for it to whisper to? And you knew the smell of the

sun and the clouds and the flying birds? Oh no, I couldn't pull off your wing. I couldn't. I couldn't."

Mona began to cry. She remembered Barbara's story and the wings that never grew beyond their little bumps; she remembered all the other ants who longed to be able to fly but would never fly because they had no wings; and here was ungrateful Queen Antonia pleading for her wings to be pulled off! It didn't seem fair. And the wedding dress was spoiled. And the cousin of the cousin of Uncle Rufus who had brought the wedding dress all the way from South America by jet hadn't been able to spare the energy to sew a tiny square of pocket in Mona's red velvet dress and she'd had to carry her plan tucked inside her sunbonnet which really wasn't a place for carrying Plans.

"Stop crying, Mona, and pull my wing off."

Mona still did not move. She had begun to sob. "And—and—it's Swarm Day and everything," she cried. "Is this what Swarm Day means, after all the picnic and that?"

"Yes, this is Swarm Day," Queen Antonia said gently. "Is this your first Swarm Day, Mona Minim?"

Mona whispered, "Yes."

"It's my second and my last Swarm Day. I didn't know how it would be either, Mona Minim. I didn't know that my lovely wedding dress would be torn and my wings would drop off or I would have to pull them off by myself, and then find a dark place to lay my eggs and have no one to talk to, and nothing to eat but my wings."

"You eat your *wings?*"

"And my wing muscles will disappear inside me and I will feed on them. I'd heard that part of the story but I thought it was a rumor. I'm a Queen now, Mona Minim, and I'm very happy."

"Happy. Without your wings!"

"Without my wings. And I'm going to found a colony. I promised Wallace, my husband."

"Wallace? He lived next door to us. I never thought he'd marry a Princess. Where is he now? Why isn't he here to help you and talk to you?"

Queen Antonia spoke in a matter-of-fact way. "I expect he will be dead in a few days."

Mona looked with horror at the callous young Queen. Her special wedding dress ruined, her wings broken and useless, and now her husband dying.

Queen Antonia understood and smiled sadly at Mona. "He dies because he won the race," she said.

"Did he know he would die so soon?" Mona asked, remembering the frightened young Wallace of the evening before: I don't want to Swarm tomorrow. I don't want to fly.

"I don't know," Queen Antonia said. "He would know and not know just as I knew and didn't know. And now, Miss Mona Minim, will you please help me with my other wing?"

Obediently, in silence, Mona helped her and then supported her as she struggled through the grass to the first stalks of the forest where together they hollowed a small tunnel in a mound of earth beneath two rocks.

"I can't go any further," Queen Antonia whispered as she prepared to say goodbye to Mona and creep down the tunnel to lay her eggs.

Just as she was saying goodbye it seemed to occur to her that Mona was a long way from the nest. Mona explained about her journey. Queen Antonia wished her good fortune and unclasping a tiny silver anklet from one of her legs she gave it to Mona.

"This is a Queen's Anklet. It was given to me by the Big Queen who said it had been given to her long ago and that it was fashioned by the first maker of trails, somewhere in *Ant*iquity."

Mona took the anklet. "What is it made of?"

"It's a scent, mingled with touch and frozen into the form of a jewel. It looks like silver but it is not mineral. The art of distilling and solidifying scent and touch has long been lost. There are very few of these left in the Ant World and all are worn by Queens. I want you to use this Anklet three times only, Mona, and then return it to an Ant Queen.

Queen Antonia closed her eyes, exhausted.

Mona took the anklet in wonderment. "Goodbye and thank you," she whispered.

And then, quickly, remembering, she asked urgently, her favorite question, "What is the smell of blue when you are flying in the sky and the smell of the sun and of the wind that never blows close to the grass and the earth? What is the smell of the sun?"

But Queen Antonia was gone and Mona was left without an answer. She looked up into the sky and saw there was no sky, only darkness and night.

13. The Return

The next morning with a swiftness that was not surprising if you remember that Mona was using the Queen's Anklet to guide her, Mona arrived at Barbara's rest-bed. She was weary and hungry and thirsty and hot. She found Barbara's rest-bed covered with fragments of dead leaves, while a violet plant with two of its flowers blooming and wide cool leaves in a shady canopy had grown up through the mossy mattress. Mona sat on the edge of the bed under one of the violet leaves with the sweet violet-perfume swirling around her. She leaned her head against the stalk. Then deftly she unknotted her ladybird handkerchief, found the remaining two sandwiches, one with honey between, the other with beetle preserve. They were stale now and the crusts curled at the edges and the beetle preserve had soaked through in a dark stain and the sandwich came to pieces when Mona picked it up but she did not particularly mind as she was so hungry and she did not even wait to clean her forelegs, used as hands, before she thrust the sandwich between her mandibles and chewed.

Ah. That was delicious.

Then she uncorked the glass dewdrop of honey and drank the dregs.

Then she unfolded her Plan: Find Discarded Clothes. Acquire House-Ant Smell.

Stooping to look under the bed she found there was no under-the-bed to get to, it was all leaves and pieces of grass and moss. Tugging with her forelegs she cleared a space and was delighted to feel and see and touch her old House-Ant clothes, still neatly folded as she had left them. A sudden happiness overcame her.

Just as she had left them?

Not quite.

"When my practice is to sleep till afternoon I prefer to sleep till afternoon," a voice said, and a tiny forest of legs waved around, and there, glaring from a bed of yellow sunbonnet and floral apron, was a gray well-armored woodlouse.

"You're sitting on my sunbonnet," Mona said. "You'll crush it."

"I'm sleeping on it," the woodlouse corrected. "It's part of the bedlinen of my multicolored bed."

"They're my clothes, you know," Mona said. "I left them here, oh, a long time ago, seasons ago. I want to wear them now to go home in."

"My dear Miss Ant..."

"Mona Minim."

"Well Mona Minim if you wore those clothes seasons ago they're not likely to fit you now are they?"

Mona was dismayed.

"I never thought of that. Let me try them and if they don't fit you can use them as bedlinen for your multicolored bed."

Reluctantly the woodlouse crept off Mona's sunbonnet and Mona noticed that he was careful not to overturn himself for then she would have had no choice but to suck the juices from his body and leave him in a shrivelled gray heap of armor. He knew this and she knew that he knew; it was the way of an ant and the way of a woodlouse.

"Here are your clothes."

Mona looked distastefully now at the floral apron, the tiny black-buttoned shoes, the yellow sunbonnet. How small they were! The flowers on the apron had faded and the black-buttoned shoes had lost their shine and two of their buttons, and the yellow sunbonnet was a dull brown color. Mona looked down at her grown ant's feet and then at the six diminutive shoes. She knew the woodlouse was right. She had outgrown her clothes. None of these would fit her.

She could acquire their smell though if they still had the smell of a little House Ant. But was that likely? Mona touched and waved her *ant*ennae; she had forgotten the House-Ant smell; even so there was no smell here but that of the ribbed gray-armored cream-bellied close-to-earth woodlouse. She would have to go home with the Garden-Ant smell upon her and risk being attacked and killed by one of the House-Ant sentries or soldiers. But they would know her, wouldn't they, even without the House-Ant smell? Of course they would know her!

While the woodlouse grumblingly retrieved the bedlinen of his multicolored bed and settled once more to sleep, Mona sat under the violet leaf and tried to remember the House Ants and Aunt Theodora and Pamela but it all seemed so long ago, and nothing was very clear, and all that was clear was her growing up among the Garden Ants. What if the sentries asked her to name well-known members of the House-Ant colony? What would she say?

She practiced to herself. "Aunt Theodora, Pamela, and—and—oh, Aunty Reepy. But then every ant's nest all over the ant world had an Aunty Reepy.

An idea came to Mona. She could mention the Stair Game. She remembered it as being a very famous game, talked of and dreamed of by every ant. Everyone would remember that and realize her House Ant-ness at once.

Smoothing her red velvet dress and adjusting her sunbonnet with the Plan inside it she left the rest-bed and considered which way she should go to the nest of the House Ants. She did not know where to turn; or rather she might not have known if she had not been given the Queen's Anklet that in her first use of it had guided her through the winding green-dappled paths of the Sunflower Forest. Mona supposed that unless the journey had been made without pause for rest or food she would have to look on the next stage of her journey as her second use of the Anklet. She would keep the third use, she decided, to find Barbara and the lost ants. She was glad it was a modern anklet and that she did not have to coax it or speak to it or chant rhymes to it as she had heard was the way with some instruments of magic. She touched the Anklet. How cold it was! She had never touched anything so cold; it was colder than the ice that made pearls out of the dewdrops and morning lightbulbs in the grass heads; nothing would ever unlock its secret senses.

Using her own trail-finding mechanism as well as the Anklet, for she did not want her senses to rust as happened in the nursery story she'd heard as an inf*ant*, she soon found the House Ant trail and was surprised and alarmed that when the smell of the House Ants was received by her *anten*-nae she could feel her abdomen arch and her mandibles prepare for killing. She was surrounded now by a smell that was alien and hostile and yet it was the smell of her own species. If a House Ant had come upon her path just then she would have been the attacker; fortunately none came and as she advanced further toward the nest she licked as much of the House-Ant smell as she could, though it sickened her to do this, and then anointed her body with it and though she had not completely rid herself of the smell of the Garden Ants she hoped that she would meet and feel less hostility.

Climbing the stairs was hard work. The trail was made at the side along the foot of the banisters and halfway up there was a tiny high-rise apartment constructed in the banisters by one of the carpenter ants that had entered the country as an illegal immigrant. Mona remembered the news of it. Hadn't it been Pamela's uncle who had marched in protest when whole families of carpenter ants had been murdered, even before they could set mandible into the country? The people called it fumigation; the ants called it murder. But one lone carpenter ant must have escaped and set up home in the new land.

Mona continued up the stairs. It was late afternoon now and it was cold in the shadow of the House and there was still not a House Ant in sight or scent. Mona was beginning to wish she had saved one of the sandwiches and a few drops of nectar. She hoped she might pass a feeding ant and persuade it to share its full stomach, but as there were no worker ants in the trail it was not likely there were feeding ants loitering around as public stomachs for hungry workers.

Taking her lawn handkerchief from her pocket Mona wiped her face and said, twice, "Whew. Whew."

Then she sat down, took off her shoes (so much bigger than the black-buttoned shoes of long ago) put on her six red resting-slippers, and rested.

Just then a black ant appeared on the trail. A worker, not a soldier.

"Hey," it called advancing with its *ant*ennae waving.

"Wait," Mona cried. "I'm a House Ant."

The stranger stood smelling and touching. He seemed undecided.

"It's O.K." he said, "as far as I can tell. Where are you going?"

"Home among the House Ants."

"Home?"

"I live here."

The worker looked doubtful. "You may have trouble with the sentries," he warned. "But good luck." He went on his way. He seemed agreeable, Mona thought. He reminded her of Nigel or Uncle Pogo. He might even be in the carrying business.

Taking off her red resting-slippers and putting on her walking shoes she continued along the trail, up and up and up, and it was sundown when she reached the top of the stairs. She recognized it at once as the top of the stairs. Why hadn't she known it on her first day out of the nest?

Here there was activity: Eggs being carried inside from their sunning-places, workers returning home with food, younger ants resting or sharing the work or playing—could it be the Stair Game?"

Two soldiers, suddenly standing before Mona, barred her way.

They advanced.

Mona recoiled.

"Please," she whispered, "I'm a House Ant."

One soldier said to the other. "Her shape's without question. She's one of us."

The other argued. "Her smell is House Ant. Her clothes are alien."

Mona looked dignified. "I've been abroad," she said. "I've traveled. These clothes are specially imported."

"That melts no honey with us," the first soldier said. "Identify yourself."

Mona lost the dignity she had adopted as a much-traveled ant.

"I'm Mona. Mona Minim."

"The nest is full of Monas. What do you work at?"

"Nursery and miscellaneous."

"Who's your family?"

"There's Aunt Theodora."

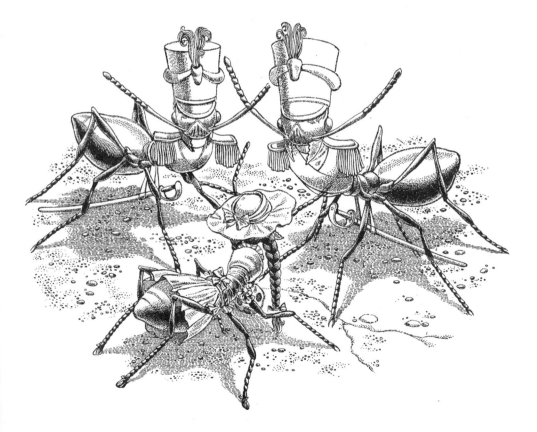

"Aunt Theodora? Who's she?"

The other soldier whispered to her companion. "You remember. She was killed in the War."

So there has been a War, Mona thought, feeling desolate.

"There's no Aunt Theodora here."

Mona felt ready to cry. Why didn't they believe her story?

"I used to know Pamela," she said. "Pamela was my best friend."

"There's only one Pamela. I'm Pamela," one of the soldiers said. "I've no friend called Mona. Except years and seasons ago there was a little ant, Mona Minim, who fell through the crack in the stairs and was killed on her first day out of the nest."

"That's me," Mona said illogically.

"But you're not killed, you're alive."

"But I wasn't killed!"

"I can see you weren't! Mona was, though. Poor Mona."

"But I'm Mona!"

Oh what was the use? Mona could see that the soldiers were getting tired of trying to identify her; they wanted action.

"Have you any other means of identification?"

Desperately Mona recalled the Stair Game. She began, hesitating, "You know. The Stair Game. The Stair Game."

Both soldiers looked blankly at her. "I know of no such game," Pamela said.

"The Stair Game," Mona pleaded.

"Really I know of no such game," Pamela said impatiently. "Though there may have been. Infants play the strangest games."

"But there *was* a Stair Game, oh a very famous game it was. You hid from Aunt Theodora and you made a false trail into the corner where the eggs were sunning, and there was tiggy and touch and hide-and-seek and then you swung on the spider-swing..."

Pamela was looking thoughtful. "There used to be a special spider-swing in the corner when I was an *infant*."

Then she came closer and smelled and touched Mona once more and then with an awakening wonder and memory she exclaimed, "Are you really the little Mona Minim who fell through the crack in the stairs on her first day out of the nest?"

"Yes," Mona whispered urgently. "Yes, yes."

If they did not believe her now they would never believe her.

Pamela's voice was gentle. "Where have you been, Mona Minim?"

"I—I—I . . ." Mona did not know what to say.

Pamela frowned and became a soldier again. "We're on duty," she said. "Go into the nest and find yourself a spare bed in our house. I live with Uncle Bill and Aunt Gloria. I'll come home later. I believe you but you'll have to be identified by a Committee tomorrow. You know what may happen if you can't prove your identity . . ."

"Yes," Mona whispered.

"Will you risk it?"

Now what would you do if you were an ant who had been walking up the stairs all day with only a honey sandwich and a beetle preserve sandwich and a few drops of nectar to drink, if you were returning home after a long absence and found that at first you were disbelieved, then half-believed, then believed but told by your former best friend that you might still be imprisoned or killed? In your own home.

Mona did what any ant might have done. She burst into tears and with her tiny bundle in the ladybird handkerchief she stumbled the few yards along the trail and into the nest, and trying not to heed the curious glances and touches of all the bustling ants who seemed so much at home yet so strange, she made her way along the corridor. She stopped a fat glowworm who was lighting his lamp for the night.

"Where does Pamela live?"

"Third from the end on the left," the glow worm answered promptly. "May I light you there and carry your luggage?"

Mona smiled gratefully at him and gave him her ladybird handkerchief.

"Here you are. Pamela lives here."

"Oh thank you."

Mona took her bundle, and thankful that the glowworm had asked no questions she walked into the house and searched until she found a room that was unoccupied, with a bed, a chest of drawers, and a huge beetle-back mirror hanging from ceiling to floor. Unpacking her luggage Mona put her best *ant*ennae brush on the table near the mirror and her spare set of clothing in one of the drawers and her six red resting-slippers under the bed.

Then still with her red velvet dress on she climbed on to the bed, drew up the coverlet that was made of some material she had never seen before— perhaps a remn*ant* of stuff from the House—and she lay a few moments trying to convince herself that she was safe and at home before she fell fast asleep.

14. The Ghost
of Uncle Pogo

*T*he next morning at a meeting of the Committee, with
Pamela as Mona's chief defend*ant*, Mona was not only officially believed to
be Mona Minim and granted her citizenship as a House Ant, she was also
acclaimed as a heroine who had survived more than ninety-nine days in the
perilous World beyond the Nest. The rescue of her friend Barbara and other
Garden Ants, the Chief of the Committee reminded her, was a personal
affair which she must carry out alone. But should she succeed she would
be granted one of the highest awards in the Ant Kingdom, as well as the
scrolled ninety-nine day survival certificate which had already been pre-
sented to her.

To Mona, after her fears of the day before, it all sounded rather pompous
and frightening. She wasn't that much of a heroine, she'd simply been
found when she was lost and now she had to find her former rescuer. There
was little heroism in that.

But there was magic!

"I'll try to find Barbara this very day, alone and unaided," she said, trying
to sound modest but aware that she sounded very heroic. She was beginning
to enjoy being a heroine.

She smiled to think that they didn't know and would never know about the Queen's Anklet.

The meeting dispersed and Mona in her clean pressed new House-Ant clothes walked calmly from the room. She felt happy. She knew that the younger ants were looking at her and saying to one another, "That's Mona Minim with her ninety-nine day Survival Certificate."

As Mona passed she smiled a slightly patronizing smile.

Yet once inside her bedroom she did not feel so confident. She knew it would be best to try to rescue Barbara at once even if only because her heroic mood was upon her! Pamela had already gone to work. Aunt Gloria and Uncle Bill were away performing their duties.

Mona sat on the edge of her bed. Suddenly she felt very lazy. Oh why did she have to rescue a Garden Ant, now, at once, when life was so comfortable and she was a heroine and had a Certificate of Survival? She reminded herself that the Garden Ant was her friend Barbara. She recalled the day that Barbara and the other ants were captured and she seemed to see once again Barbara's frightened face pressed against the glass of the Ant Farm walls. And then to herself she tried to revive her plea that she was Mona Minim, too small to rescue imprisoned ants; not able to find the way; frightened; new, not long out of the nest.

What a long time ago it seemed. She was still small, Mona Minim, but she was grown up and had survived ninety-nine days in the World, and Barbara was captured and languishing somewhere in an Ant Farm prison.

"I'll go now," Mona thought. "I'll go now and rescue Barbara and the other ants."

In her imagination she saw herself again before the Committee. She was dressed in a new glossy gray moth-fur coat and receiving the Highest Award in the Ant Kingdom, the Scroll of Bravery . . .

But in the midst of her dreaming she thought suddenly of Uncle Pogo and she knew that if he could read her thoughts he would make joking remarks. He would say, "Don't mind my *bant*er. I don't want to be *ant*agonistic but, little Mona Minim, you have a *fant*astic imagination!"

15. An Anklet for a Queen

*T*aking the anklet for the third and last time it could be used Mona found herself guided as if by magic, and it *was* magic, up through the crack in the beams of the garage roof, along the kitchen floor of the house in the crack between the floor and the wall, under the linoleum, across a corridor and into a room, along beside the wall, beneath a piece of furniture, approaching the window and then up, up the wall, groping, careful, to the jutting windowsill and over the windowsill into a bath of light where in the shade provided by the curtain, the glass-walled house that was the Ant Farm was standing. The journey, in thinking-time so short, had taken Mona almost three hours. She was tired and hungry and thirsty and in her eagerness to carry out the rescue she had forgotten to bring food or drink. Wiping her brow with her clean lawn handkerchief she leaned against the curtain and dozed a little. Clearly, the boy of the house, Peter, was nowhere within sight or smell or touch.

Half an hour later Mona woke up in some alarm, not remembering where she was and how she came to be leaning against the folds of a curtain. Then she remembered. She knew that she had fallen asleep partly because she was so tired and partly because she had not been able to face the thought of crawling toward the Ant Farm and seeing poor Barbara within it, a wasted prisoner. Or she might not even be alive!

Mona felt her heart beating fast as she made her way toward the glass-walled Farm.

She arrived. Her *ant*ennae explored the glass, knocking and tapping and in beams of light reflected within the glass so that she too seemed to be captured. She looked at the shadow of herself that crawled wherever she crawled and tapped and knocked when she tapped and knocked. Then she blinked her eyes and opening them again she found herself gazing directly into an Ant's Nest or how an Ant's Nest would appear if the earth surrounding it were transparent. She identified the various tunnels and chambers; the store room, packed with food; the cemetery, neatly sprinkled with sand; the quarters of the different families. Then Mona was aware of ants hurrying to and fro, working, meeting, communicating, gossiping, bustling, as ants would do in any well-ordered nest. She did not know if she recognized any of the Garden Ants, though she peered close to the walls, noting first one ant, then another, but unable even to recognize Barbara. It's no use, she thought. Barbara must have died long ago. And I never rescued her because I was just little Mona Minim, too small and new and not able to find my way.

Sadly she turned and was about to leave the Ant Farm when she found herself gazing into yet another room in the nest, the room where the Princess lived. The Princess looked very handsome there on her thistledown bed with its fancy bedlight with the gnat's-wing shade, and servants hurrying about attending to her every need, anointing her body, washing, perfuming . . . and what a fine pair of wings she had, how delicate yet strong. As Mona stared at this unexpected view of the toilet of a Princess she suddenly shook her head wildly and gasped with astonishment.

The Princess was Barbara!

But it couldn't be!

But it was!

Mona tapped frantically on the wall· and Barbara hearing the muffled sound looked up and saw Mona but did not at first recognize her. Then to the alarm of her maids Barbara began to crawl from the room, along the tunnel and up up to the entrance to the nest, near the roof of the Farm, while Mona, following, crawled up the outside of the glass until she too was soon near the roof-entrance. She was surprised to see that there was ample space for any ant to escape. Why hadn't Barbara and the others—if there were others—escaped?

Touching, combing *ant*ennae for messages, excitedly gossipping ...

But all Mona could say was, "You are really a princess. You are really a princess."

Barbara explained. "I was captured because I looked big enough to be a future Queen. I don't know where the others are. They were not brought to the Ant Farm with me. But I was taken here and chosen as the Princess because I am big and strong, and so my wings ..." she laughed delightedly, jerking her shoulders; her wings made a soft whirring sound as she moved— "and so my wings grew. You know what it's like with ants. If the colony wants you to become a future Queen you become one; you even grow wings. All the members of the colony are Garden Ants, distant relations—there was no scent hostility at all, though a few died in the first testing battles. Oh Mona Minim, you can almost do anything in the ant world if the colony wants it, can't you? Remember old Aunty Flo?

Mona had heard jokes about Aunty Flo but she did not know her story. Barbara told how she was an old-maid crotchety member of the Chewing Society who suddenly laid eggs and had male children simply because she was so worried by the shortage of workers.

"It's a miracle," Mona said, this time without envy for she knew, though she did not know if Barbara knew, of the fate of wings in the life of an ant. "Isn't it?"

Barbara was twisting and turning and whirring her wings.

"And you've never wanted to escape then?"

"Oh no, it's wonderful here. It would take days and days to tell you."

Mona frowned. "I don't think I'd like it," she said.

Then Barbara wanted to know about Mona and how she had found the Ant Farm and whether she was living with the Garden Ants.

And how was Uncle Pogo?

And Cousin Nigel?

And Aunt Phyllis?

And did the Princess have her Naming Day?

"Antonia," Mona said quietly. She found she was not listening now. She stooped down and unclasping the Queen's Anklet she gave it to Barbara.

Without mentioning Antonia she told Barbara about the Anklet and how it was to be used three times and then given to a Queen.

"It has had its third using and you are to be Queen!"

How happy Barbara appeared! But suddenly she frowned and whispered, "Mona, Mona, perhaps you had better go now, the boy comes to feed us, you can come to talk to me again before I fly away. Oh isn't it wonderful to have wings, to fly and know the smell of the blue in the sky, of the

wind that never comes close to the earth grass but blows, I think, among the heavenly grasses; to fly and know the smell of the sun—remember?"

"Yes, I remember."

"You could have grown wings too, if they had brought you here," Barbara said gently, not understanding the sad expression on Mona's face.

Mona did not answer. Then the two said goodbye and quickly Mona crawled down the wall to the crack between the floor and the wall and toward the door of Peter's bedroom.

But the trail was long and difficult. She no longer had the Queen's Anklet. She had forgotten that she would need to find her own way home. Fortunately she was no longer little Mona Minim on her first day out of the nest!

There was one frightening moment when the door opened suddenly and knocked her sideways as she was setting out to cross the corridor to the kitchen. She felt dazed and sick. She did not think she would be able to crawl all that way across the corridor, in the open, without a sheltering crack between the floor and the wall. She felt that she had little strength left.

She was never able to understand how she arrived home. It seemed like magic, but this time it was not. Crawling and limping and trying to discover the slight scent she had left on her outward journey she at last arrived at the entrance of the nest, and there fell unconscious, and half-recovered to find herself being put to bed, and there were ants bending over her and whispering and then she saw her reflection as if in a wall of glass and her *ant*ennae were knocking against the wall, and she was crying, "I don't want to go to the Ant Farm, I don't want to go to the Ant Farm."

And Barbara was there, smiling and shaking her wings. "I like it here," she said. "And when I fly, when I fly..." But it was not Barbara, it was Queen Antonia, and then it was Wallace and Nigel and Uncle Pogo.

And then Mona was lying asleep between cool sheets and looking up at the sky, at all the whirling golden black-hearted flowers in the Sunflower Forest.

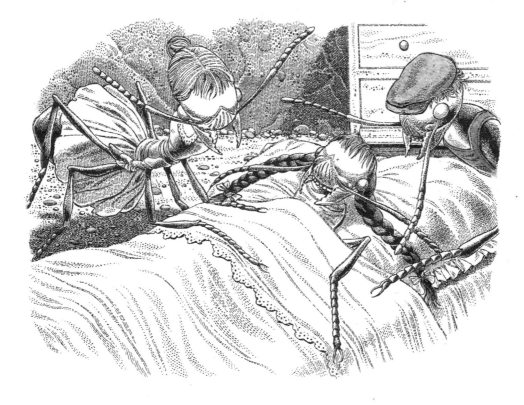

16. Mona Minim

and the Smell of

the Sun

"I'm off to sentry duty. I daresay you'll want to get up later and explore your old haunts. See you tonight."

"I'm off to sentry duty."

The words echoed in Mona's mind as she lay in bed the next morning. She thought of Aunt Phyllis and Uncle Pogo and Barbara and Nigel; of her sore scent-cone and the spider sandwiches with the crusts cut off and the warm nectar and the fondant twice a day; and she thought of the Ant Farm descending from the wintry sky; and the missed Naming Feast; and Uncle Pogo's stories.

Once upon a time, not long ago, almost now, there was a little House Ant called Mona Minim. It was her first day out of the nest...

She thought of Swarm Day and the young Queen Antonia with her broken wings. And young Wallace who didn't want to fly in the Swarm. And Mona's thinking was morning-thinking and not the night-thinking that comes when you are tired and sick. She felt happy. She remembered her visit to Barbara. Everyone would think she had failed in her rescue and she could never tell them otherwise. She would not be a heroine now and receive the Highest Award in the Ant Kingdom. She would not have to pretend to be braver than she was. And some day she would visit the Garden Ants and tell them her story and she would compile her personal *ant*hology of her experiences in both nests.

Beginning now.

There were so many things to do.

She got up. She washed and dressed. She walked along the corridor in what Pamela had described as her "old haunts." And though she remembered little of them she enjoyed their smell and she stopped to drink honey from an old Aunty Reepy who stood fat as a barrel in the corner.

But she did not go down to the egg chamber and she did not seek out the young Princess who, she supposed, would be worrying about her wedding dress for next week's Swarm Day; nor did she ask which of the young males were flying in the Swarm; and she said nothing when she passed a group of young ants whose entire conversation seemed to be about wings, their longing for wings, their envy of the young Princess and her beautiful wings. She overheard a piping voice, "I wonder what is the smell of blue and the smell of the winds that blow so high they never come near the grass of the earth, and the smell of the clouds and of being close to the sun?"

Mona was just about to say aloud, as she used to say when Uncle Pogo told his stories, "Why, that's me, little Mona Minim only two days out of the nest," when she realized that finally she was no longer little Mona Minim.

Who was she then?

Why, she was Aunt Mona. She heard the young ants whispering among themselves, "You know, Aunt Mona, who spends her time compiling the *ant*hology, who's very brave but not too brave. Aunt Mona. She's so old that no one knows when she was born."

And then Mona heard the ants turn once again to their talk of wings and flying. "What is the smell of blue in the sky, of the wind that never blows near the grass of the earth, of the clouds and the birds that fly? What is the smell of the sun?"

Mona was silent. She fancied she heard the Big Queen answering, "You must go out, little ants, and see and smell and taste and touch for yourselves and then you will know."